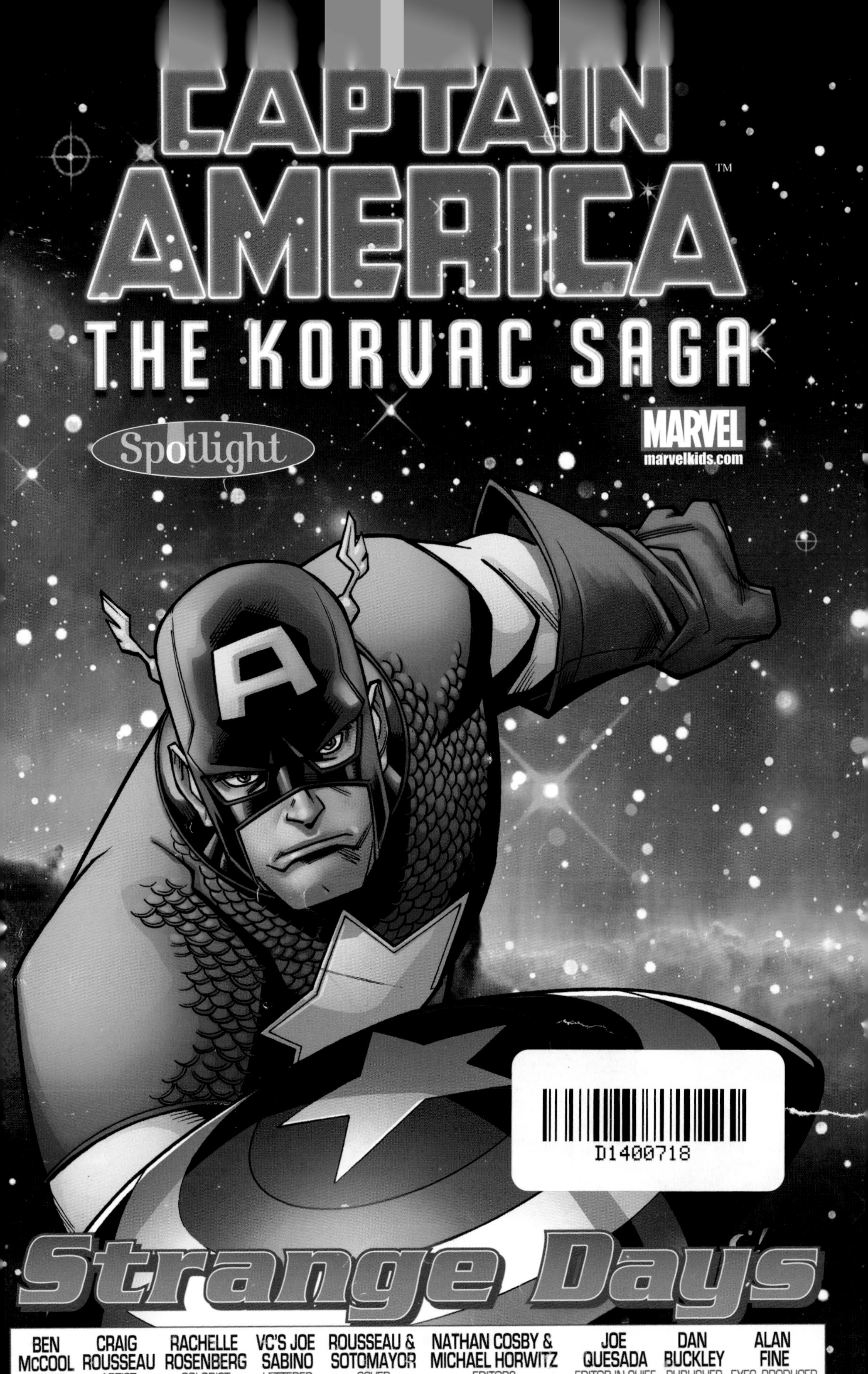
CAPTAIN AMERICA™
THE KORVAC SAGA
Spotlight
MARVEL
marvelkids.com
Strange Days



| | | | | | | | | |
|---|---|---|---|---|---|---|---|---|
| BEN McCOOL | CRAIG ROUSSEAU | RACHELLE ROSENBERG | VC'S JOE SABINO | ROUSSEAU & SOTOMAYOR | NATHAN COSBY & MICHAEL HORWITZ | JOE QUESADA | DAN BUCKLEY | ALAN FINE |
| WRITER | ARTIST | COLORIST | LETTERER | COVER | EDITORS | EDITOR IN CHIEF | PUBLISHER | EXEC. PRODUCER |

**visit us at www.abdopublishing.com**

Reinforced library bound edition published in 2013 by Spotlight, a division of the ABDO Group, PO Box 398166, Minneapolis, MN 55439. Spotlight produces high-quality reinforced library bound editions for schools and libraries. Published by agreement with Marvel Entertainment, LLC. The stories, characters, and incidents mentioned are entirely fictional. All rights reserved. Used under authorization.

Printed in the United States of America, North Mankato, Minnesota.
052012
092012
♻ This book contains at least 10% recycled materials.

TM & © 2012 Marvel & Subs.

All Rights Reserved. No part of this book may be reproduced or transmitted in any form or by any means, electronic or mechanical, including photocopying, recording, or by any information storage and retrieval system, without written permission from the publisher.

**Library of Congress Cataloging-in-Publication Data**

McCool, Ben.
  Captain America : the Korvac saga / story by Ben McCool ; art by Craig Rousseau. -- Reinforced library bound ed.
    <v. 1-> cm.
  "Marvel."
  Summary: Captain America, a proud member of the Avengers, is still trying to find his way in a strange new world when he discovers his connection to a mysterious man named Korvac, who claims to be similarly displaced in time.
  Contents: [v. 1]. Strange days --
  ISBN 978-1-61479-019-8 (Strange days: #1 : alk. paper) -- ISBN 978-1-61479-020-4 (Souljacker: #2 : alk. paper) -- ISBN 978-1-61479-021-1 (The traveler: #3 : alk. paper) -- ISBN 978-1-61479-022-8 (The star lord: #4 : alk. paper)
  1. Graphic novels. [1. Graphic novels. 2. Superheroes--Fiction. 3. Space and time--Fiction.] I. Rousseau, Craig, ill. II. Title.
  PZ7.7.M415Cap 2012
  741.5'973--dc23
                                    2012000931
ISBN 978-1-61479-019-8 (reinforced library edition)

All Spotlight books are reinforced library binding
and manufactured in the United States of America.

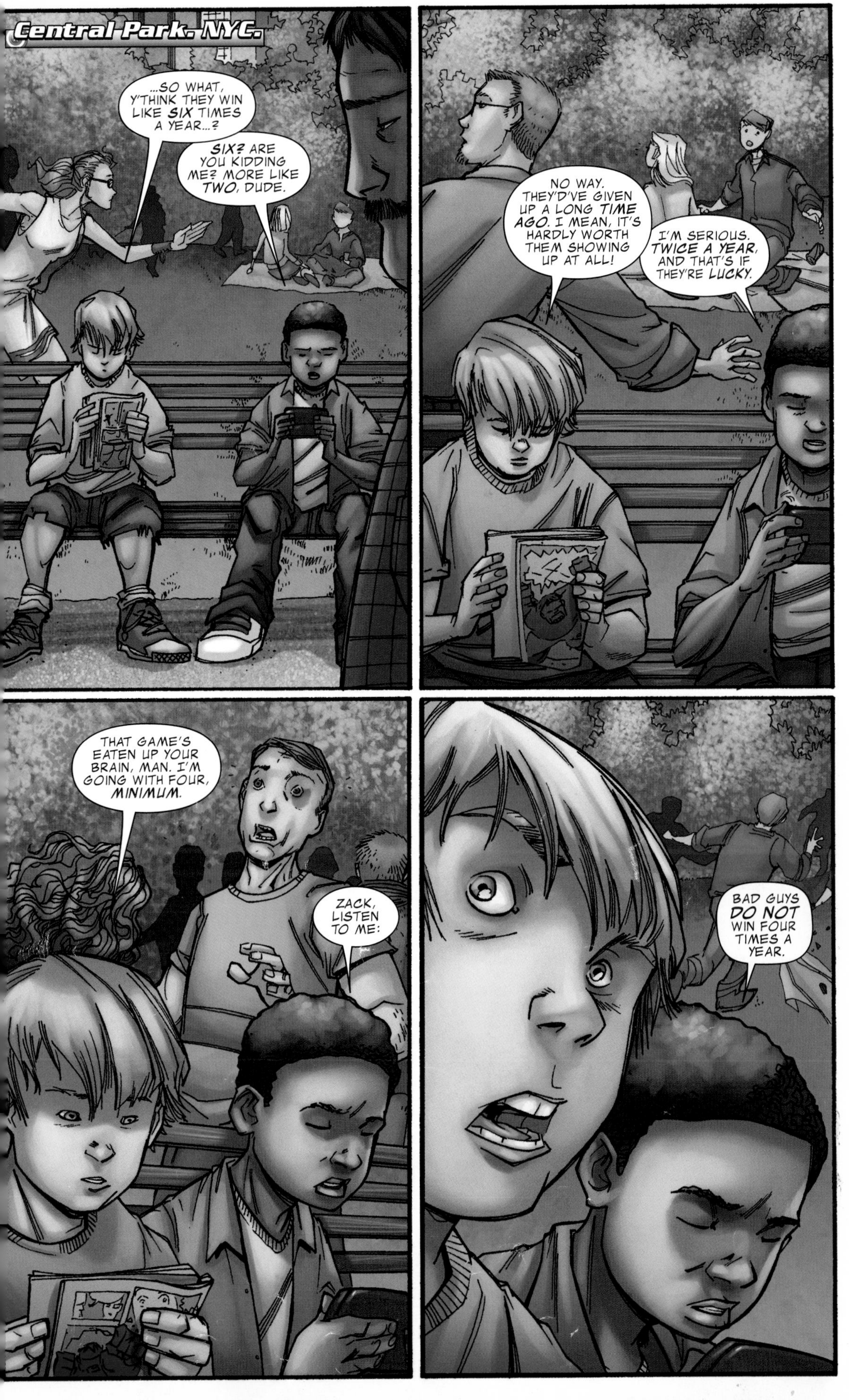
Central Park, NYC.
...SO WHAT, Y'THINK THEY WIN LIKE SIX TIMES A YEAR...?
SIX? ARE YOU KIDDING ME? MORE LIKE TWO, DUDE.
NO WAY. THEY'D'VE GIVEN UP A LONG TIME AGO. I MEAN, IT'S HARDLY WORTH THEM SHOWING UP AT ALL!
I'M SERIOUS. TWICE A YEAR, AND THAT'S IF THEY'RE LUCKY.
THAT GAME'S EATEN UP YOUR BRAIN, MAN. I'M GOING WITH FOUR, MINIMUM.
ZACK, LISTEN TO ME:
BAD GUYS DO NOT WIN FOUR TIMES A YEAR.

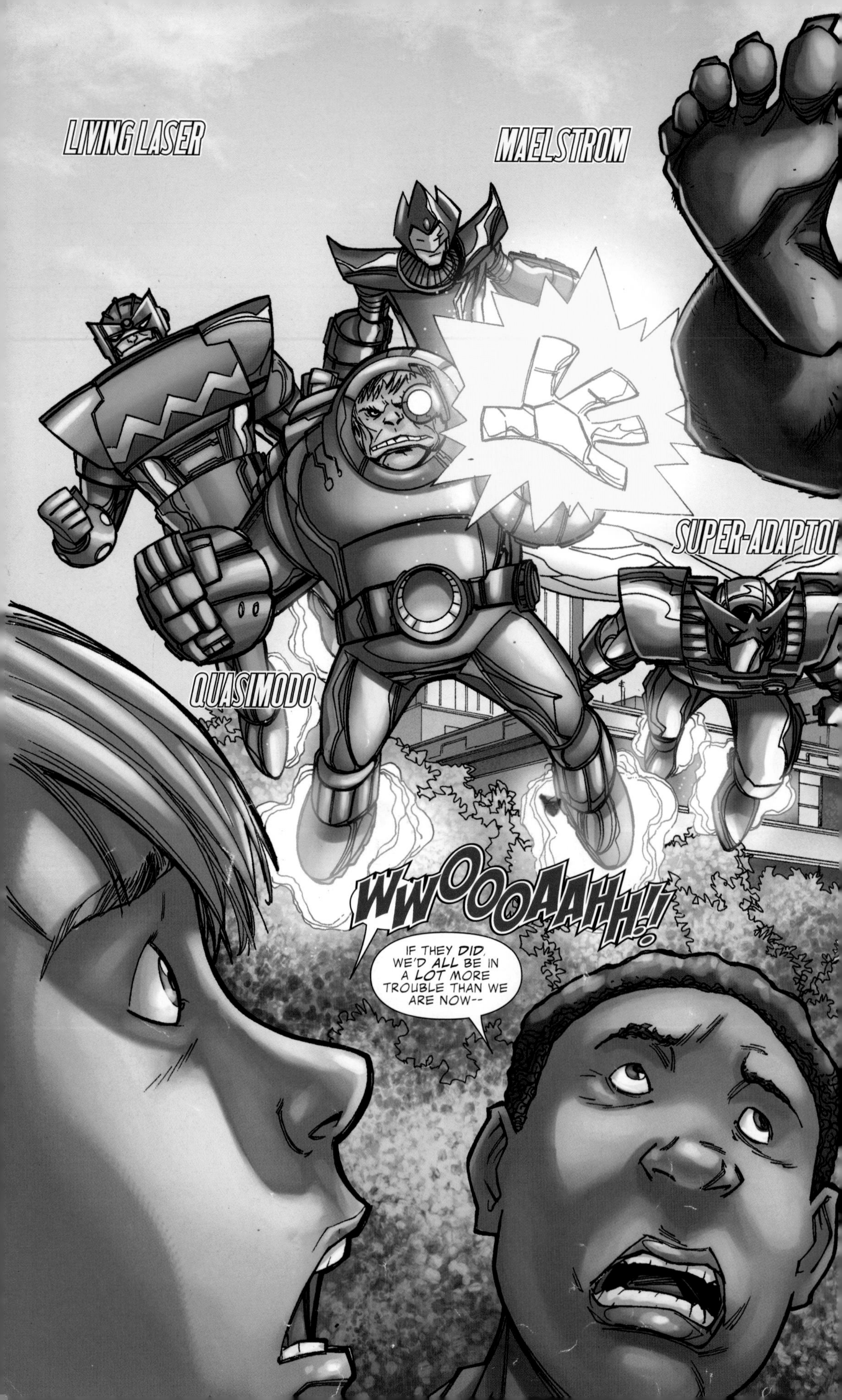
LIVING LASER
MAELSTROM
SUPER-ADAPTOI
QUASIMODO
WWOOOOAAHH!!
IF THEY DID, WE'D ALL BE IN A LOT MORE TROUBLE THAN WE ARE NOW--

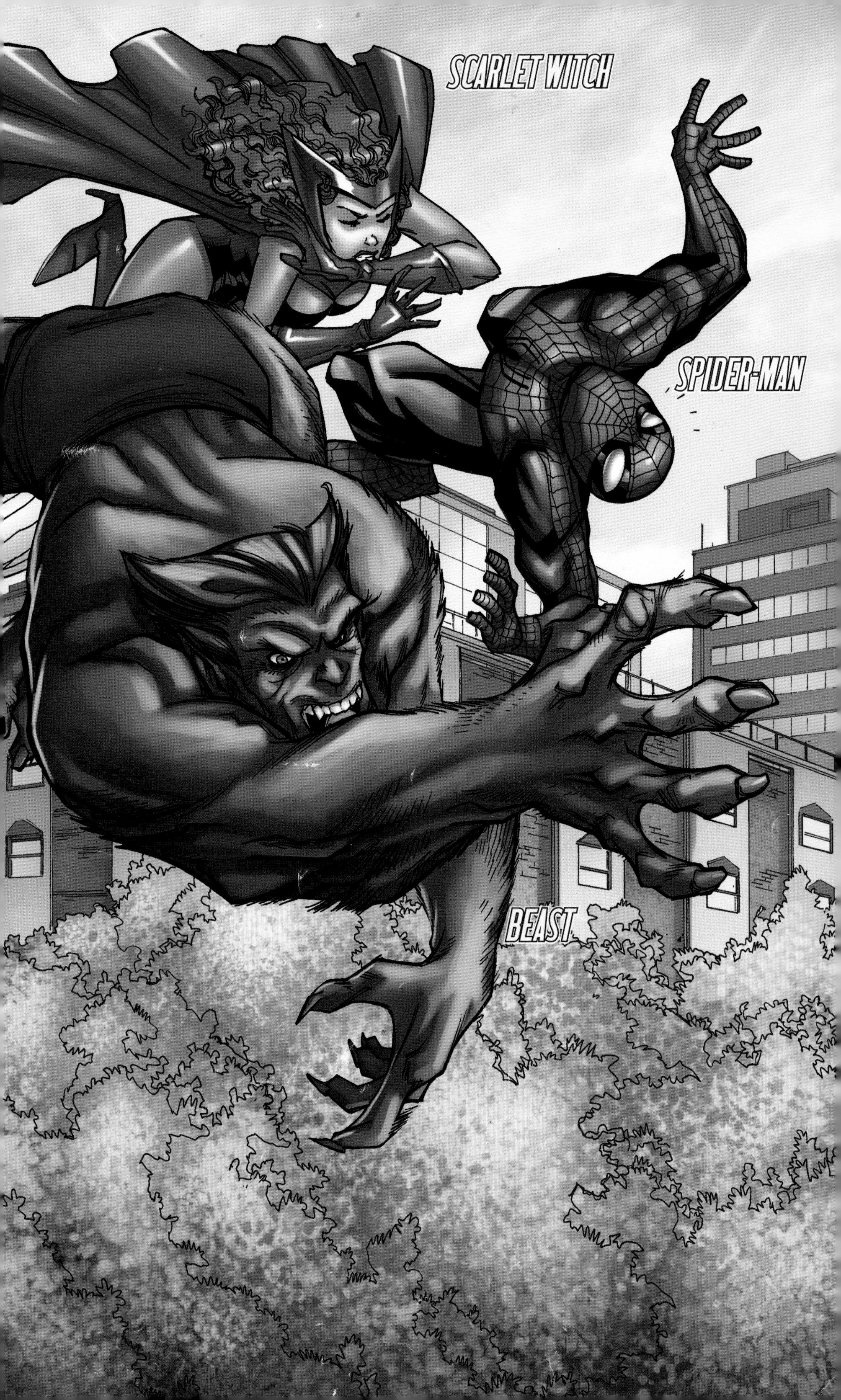
SCARLET WITCH
SPIDER-MAN
BEAST

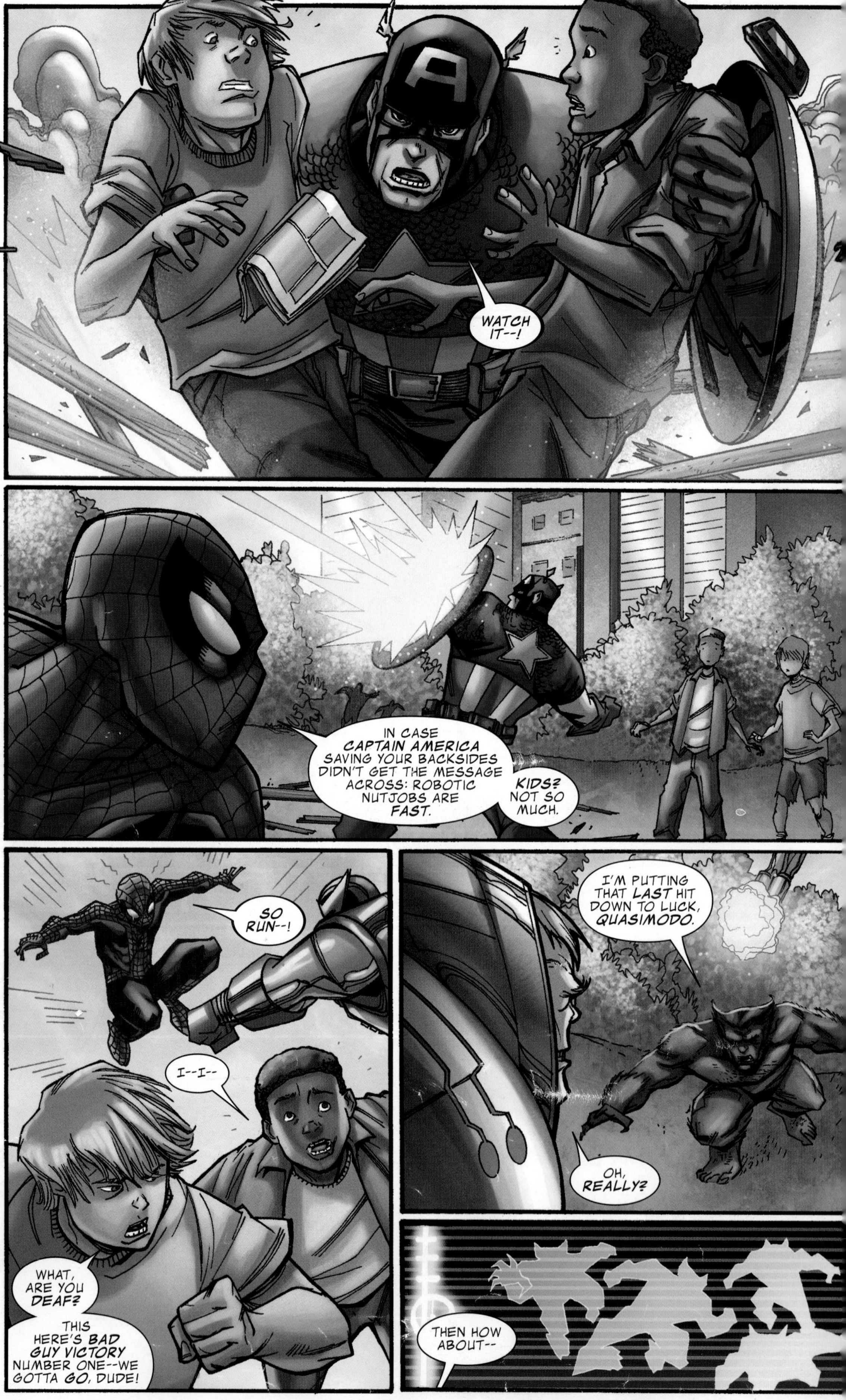
WATCH IT--!
IN CASE CAPTAIN AMERICA SAVING YOUR BACKSIDES DIDN'T GET THE MESSAGE ACROSS: ROBOTIC NUTJOBS ARE FAST.
KIDS? NOT SO MUCH.
SO RUN--!
I--I--
WHAT, ARE YOU DEAF?
THIS HERE'S BAD GUY VICTORY NUMBER ONE--WE GOTTA GO, DUDE!
I'M PUTTING THAT LAST HIT DOWN TO LUCK, QUASIMODO.
OH, REALLY?
THEN HOW ABOUT--

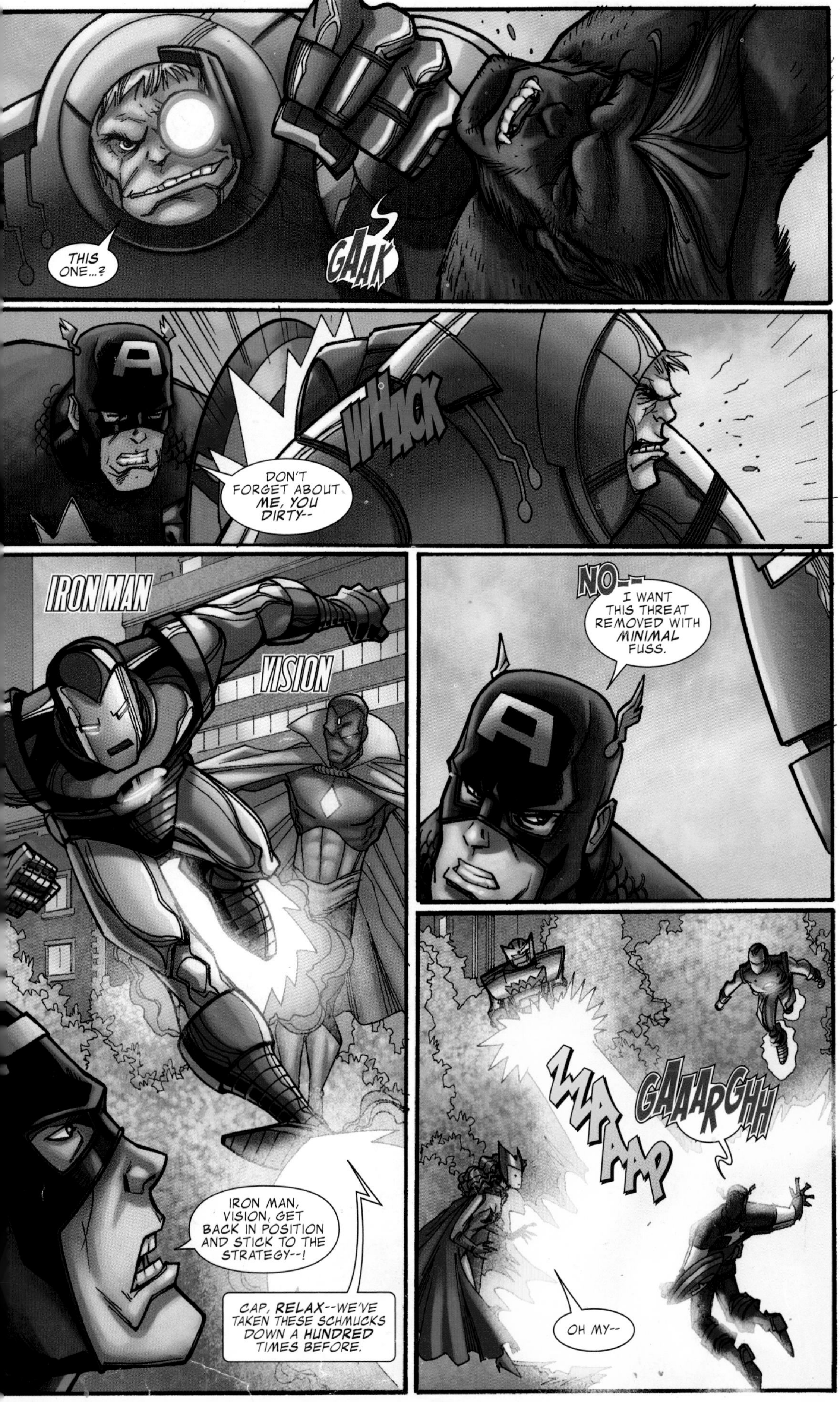
THIS ONE...?
GAAK
WHACK
DON'T FORGET ABOUT ME, YOU DIRTY--
IRON MAN
VISION
NO--
I WANT THIS THREAT REMOVED WITH MINIMAL FUSS.
IRON MAN, VISION, GET BACK IN POSITION AND STICK TO THE STRATEGY--!
CAP, RELAX--WE'VE TAKEN THESE SCHMUCKS DOWN A HUNDRED TIMES BEFORE.
ZZAAP
GAAARGHH
OH MY--

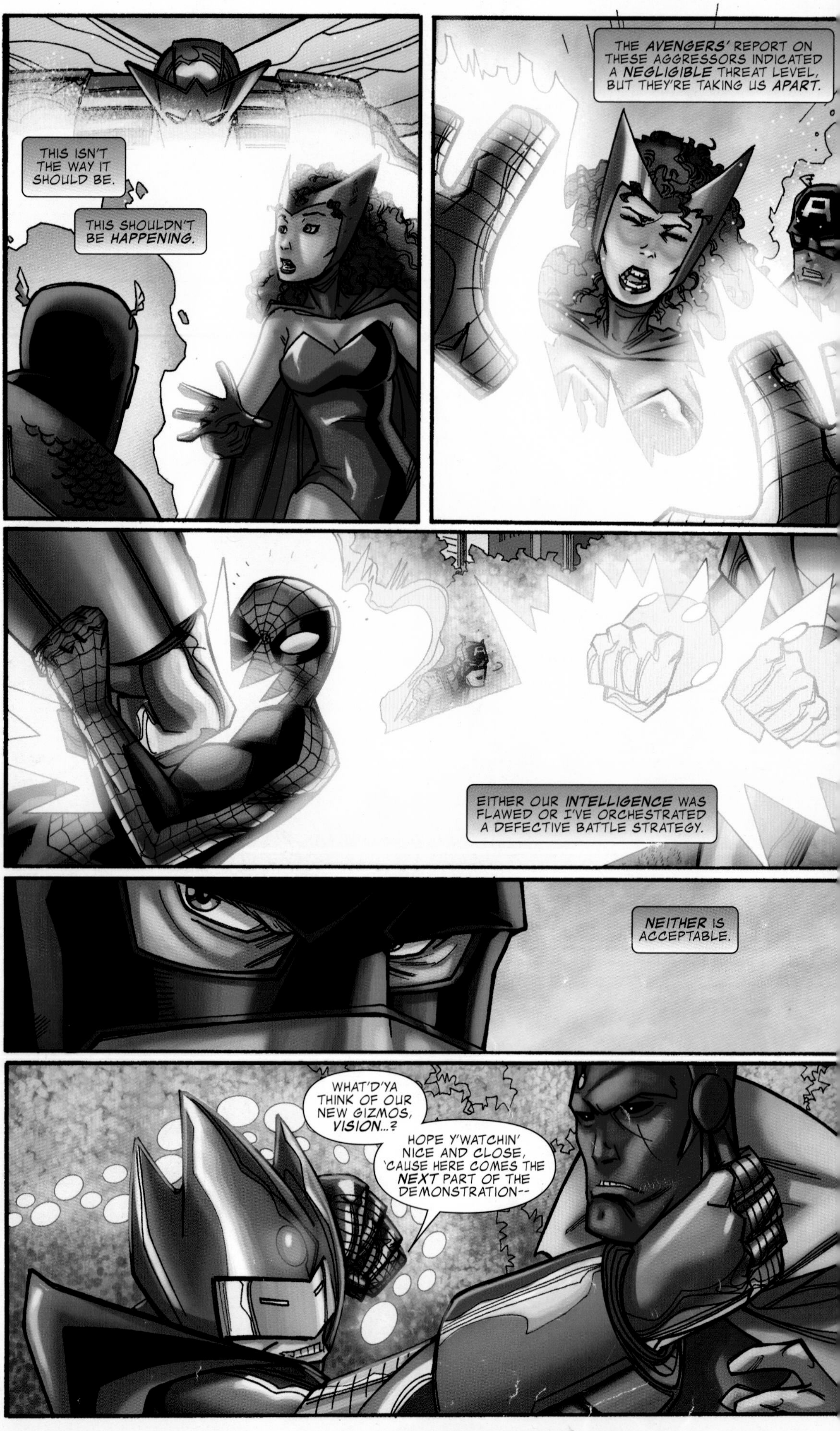
THIS ISN'T THE WAY IT SHOULD BE.
THIS SHOULDN'T BE *HAPPENING.*
THE *AVENGERS'* REPORT ON THESE AGGRESSORS INDICATED A *NEGLIGIBLE* THREAT LEVEL, BUT THEY'RE TAKING US *APART.*
EITHER OUR *INTELLIGENCE* WAS FLAWED OR I'VE ORCHESTRATED A DEFECTIVE BATTLE STRATEGY.
*NEITHER* IS ACCEPTABLE.
WHAT'D'YA THINK OF OUR NEW GIZMOS, *VISION*...?
HOPE Y'WATCHIN' NICE AND CLOSE, 'CAUSE HERE COMES THE *NEXT* PART OF THE DEMONSTRATION--

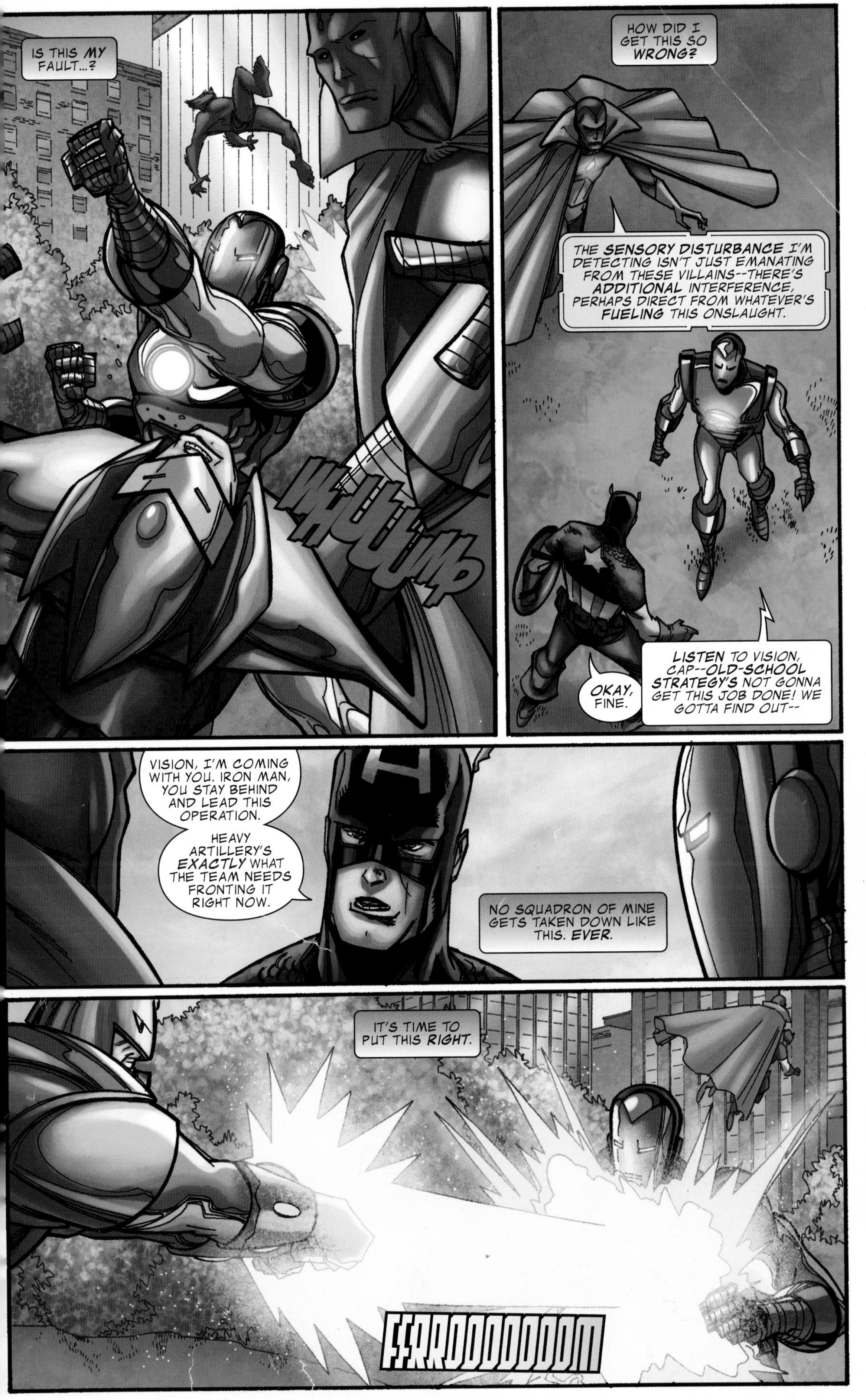
IS THIS *MY* FAULT...?
WHUMP
HOW DID I GET THIS SO *WRONG?*
THE **SENSORY DISTURBANCE** I'M DETECTING ISN'T JUST EMANATING FROM THESE VILLAINS--THERE'S **ADDITIONAL** INTERFERENCE, PERHAPS DIRECT FROM WHATEVER'S **FUELING** THIS ONSLAUGHT.
**LISTEN** TO VISION, CAP--**OLD-SCHOOL STRATEGY'S** NOT GONNA GET THIS JOB DONE! WE GOTTA FIND OUT--
OKAY, FINE.
VISION, I'M COMING WITH YOU. IRON MAN, YOU STAY BEHIND AND LEAD THIS OPERATION.
HEAVY ARTILLERY'S ***EXACTLY*** WHAT THE TEAM NEEDS FRONTING IT RIGHT NOW.
NO SQUADRON OF MINE GETS TAKEN DOWN LIKE THIS. ***EVER.***
IT'S TIME TO PUT THIS *RIGHT.*
FSRROOOOOOOM

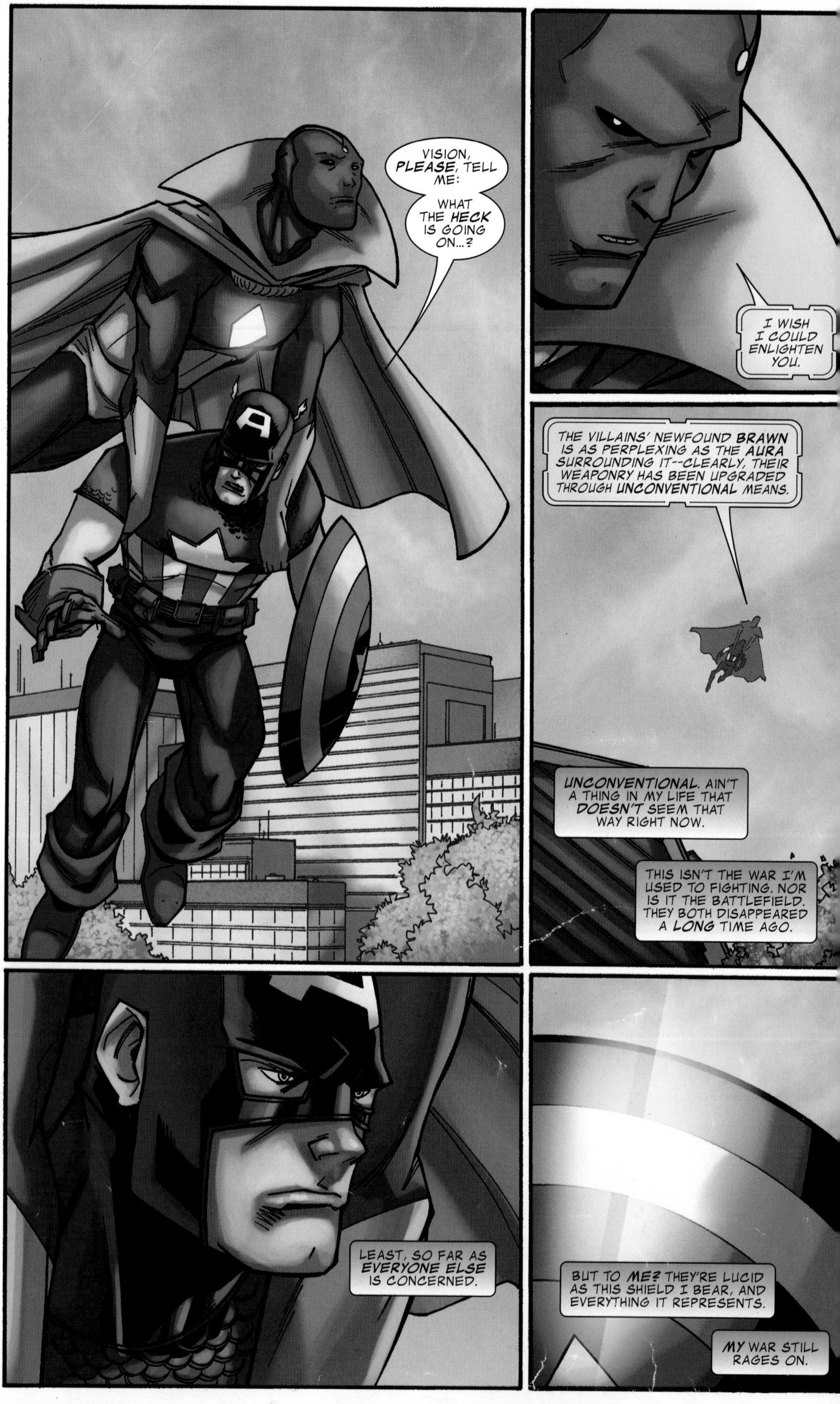
VISION, PLEASE, TELL ME:
WHAT THE HECK IS GOING ON...?
I WISH I COULD ENLIGHTEN YOU.
THE VILLAINS' NEWFOUND BRAWN IS AS PERPLEXING AS THE AURA SURROUNDING IT--CLEARLY, THEIR WEAPONRY HAS BEEN UPGRADED THROUGH UNCONVENTIONAL MEANS.
UNCONVENTIONAL. AIN'T A THING IN MY LIFE THAT DOESN'T SEEM THAT WAY RIGHT NOW.
THIS ISN'T THE WAR I'M USED TO FIGHTING. NOR IS IT THE BATTLEFIELD. THEY BOTH DISAPPEARED A LONG TIME AGO.
LEAST, SO FAR AS EVERYONE ELSE IS CONCERNED.
BUT TO ME? THEY'RE LUCID AS THIS SHIELD I BEAR, AND EVERYTHING IT REPRESENTS.
MY WAR STILL RAGES ON.

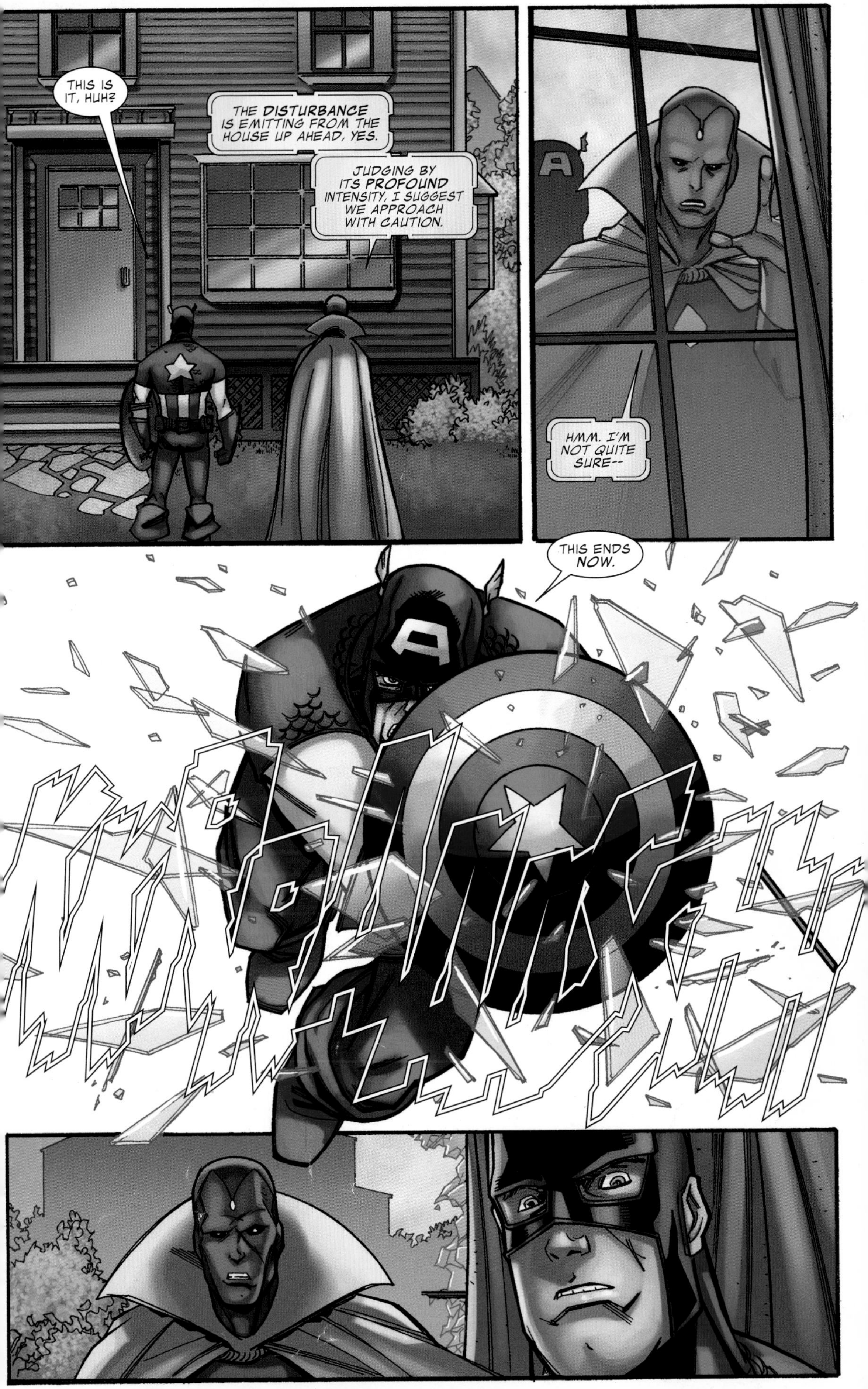
THIS IS IT, HUH?
THE DISTURBANCE IS EMITTING FROM THE HOUSE UP AHEAD, YES.
JUDGING BY ITS PROFOUND INTENSITY, I SUGGEST WE APPROACH WITH CAUTION.
HMM. I'M NOT QUITE SURE--
THIS ENDS NOW.

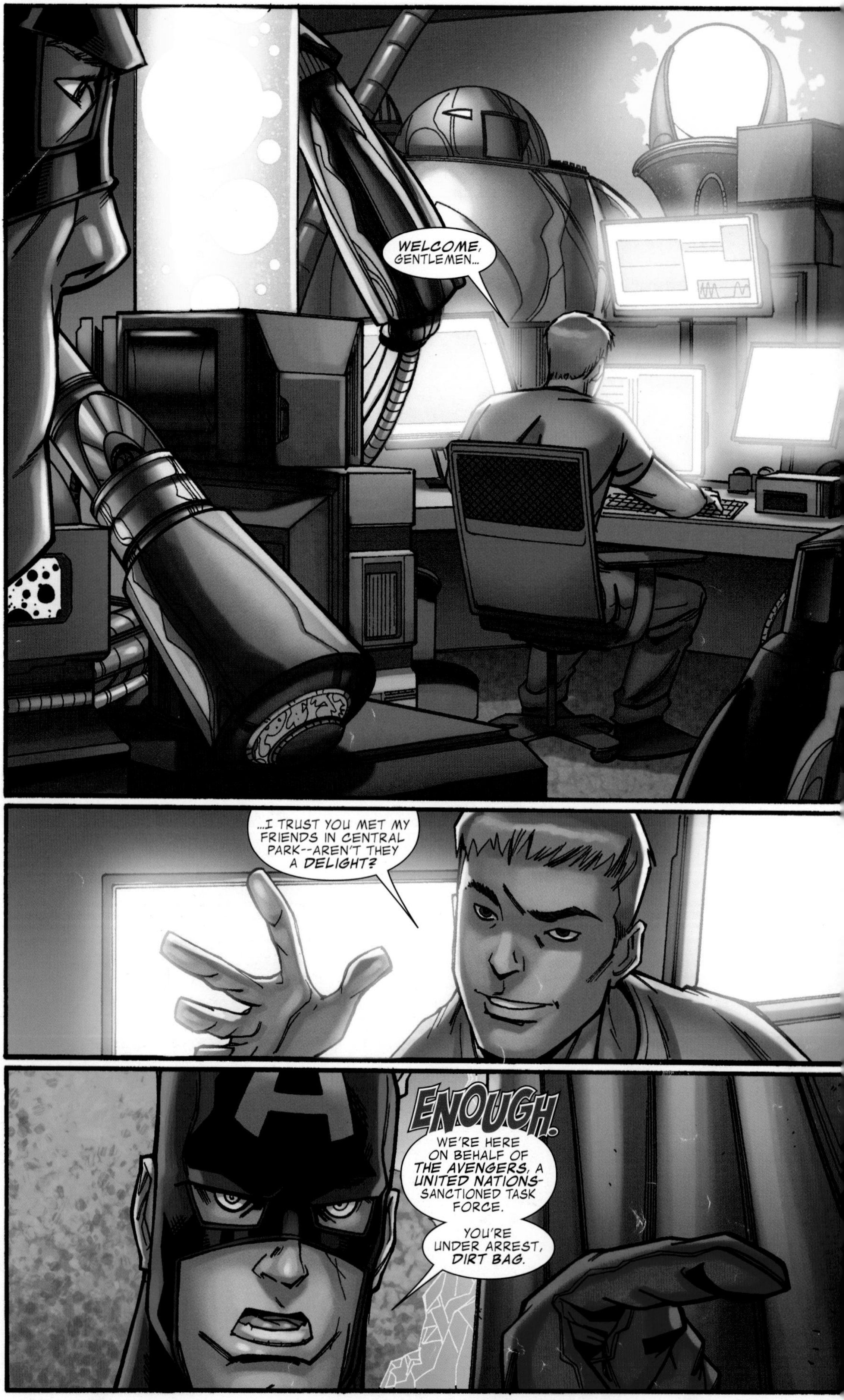
WELCOME, GENTLEMEN...
...I TRUST YOU MET MY FRIENDS IN CENTRAL PARK--AREN'T THEY A DELIGHT?
ENOUGH.
WE'RE HERE ON BEHALF OF THE AVENGERS, A UNITED NATIONS-SANCTIONED TASK FORCE.
YOU'RE UNDER ARREST, DIRT BAG.

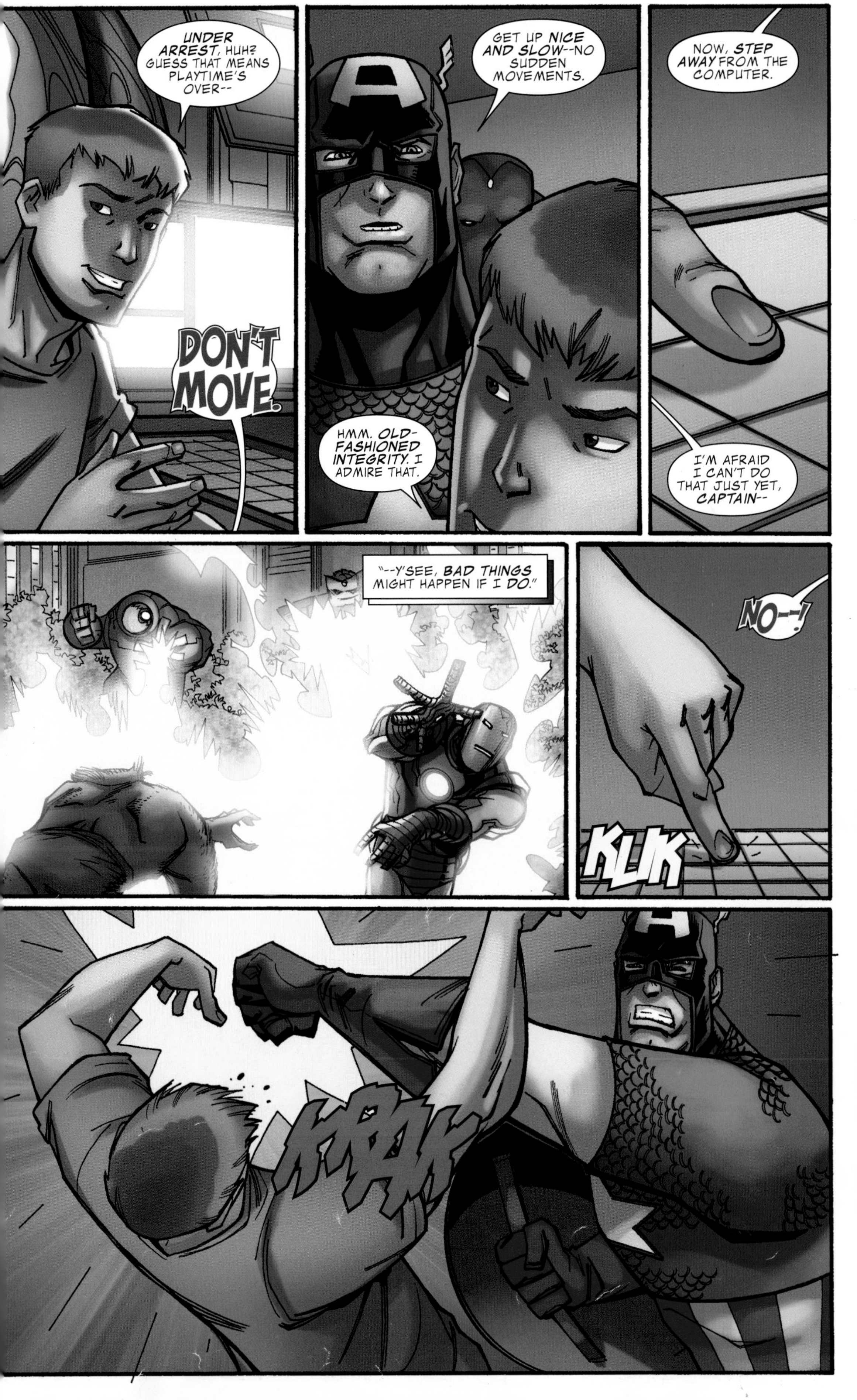
UNDER ARREST, HUH? GUESS THAT MEANS PLAYTIME'S OVER--
DON'T MOVE.
GET UP NICE AND SLOW--NO SUDDEN MOVEMENTS.
HMM. OLD-FASHIONED INTEGRITY. I ADMIRE THAT.
NOW, STEP AWAY FROM THE COMPUTER.
I'M AFRAID I CAN'T DO THAT JUST YET, CAPTAIN--
"--Y'SEE, BAD THINGS MIGHT HAPPEN IF I DO."
NO--!
KLIK
KRAK

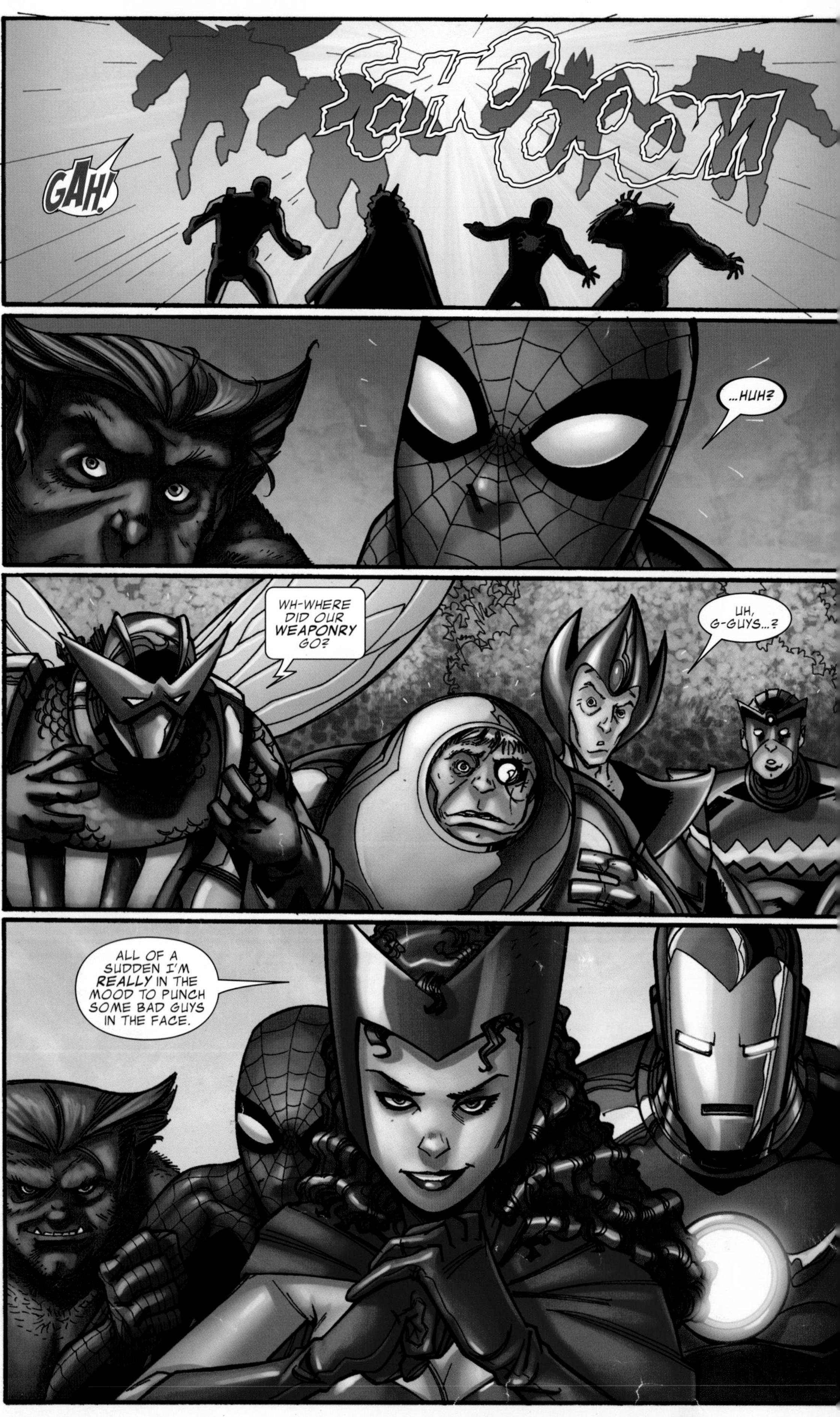
KA-BOOOM
GAH!
...HUH?
WH-WHERE DID OUR WEAPONRY GO?
UH, G-GUYS...?
ALL OF A SUDDEN I'M REALLY IN THE MOOD TO PUNCH SOME BAD GUYS IN THE FACE.

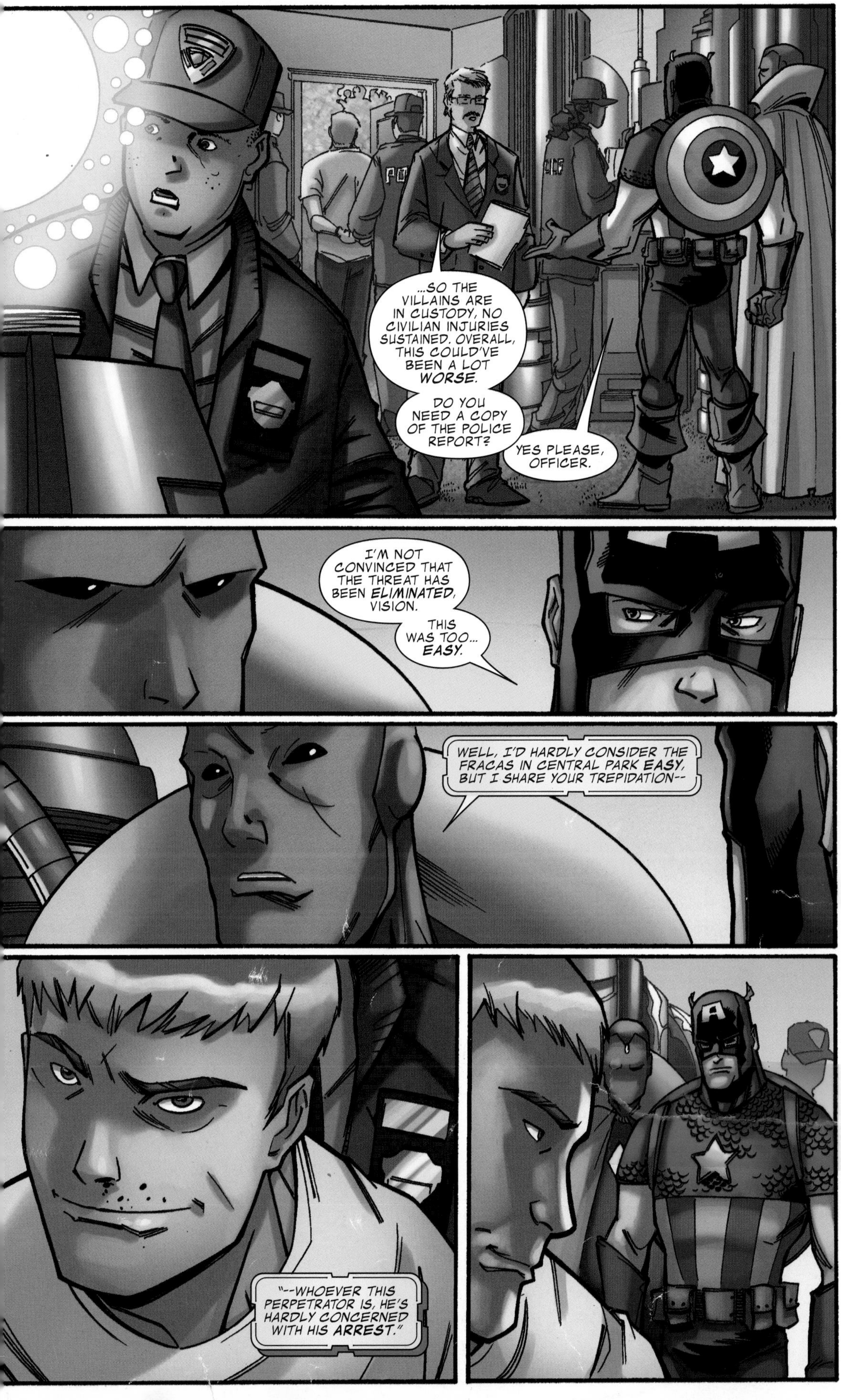
...SO THE VILLAINS ARE IN CUSTODY, NO CIVILIAN INJURIES SUSTAINED. OVERALL, THIS COULD'VE BEEN A LOT WORSE.
DO YOU NEED A COPY OF THE POLICE REPORT?
YES PLEASE, OFFICER.
I'M NOT CONVINCED THAT THE THREAT HAS BEEN ELIMINATED, VISION.
THIS WAS TOO... EASY.
WELL, I'D HARDLY CONSIDER THE FRACAS IN CENTRAL PARK EASY, BUT I SHARE YOUR TREPIDATION--
"--WHOEVER THIS PERPETRATOR IS, HE'S HARDLY CONCERNED WITH HIS ARREST."

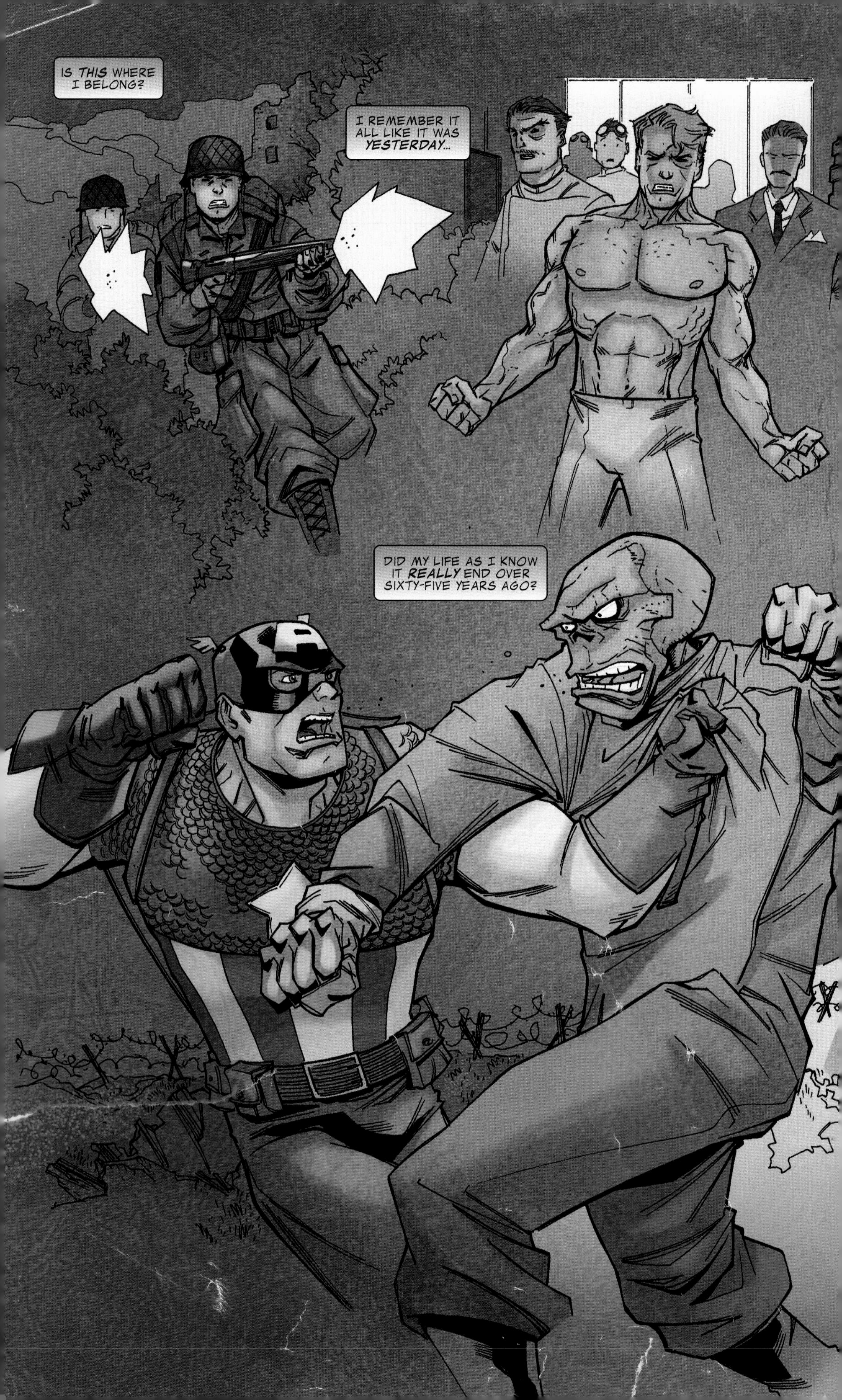
IS *THIS* WHERE I BELONG?
I REMEMBER IT ALL LIKE IT WAS *YESTERDAY*...
DID MY LIFE AS I KNOW IT *REALLY* END OVER SIXTY-FIVE YEARS AGO?

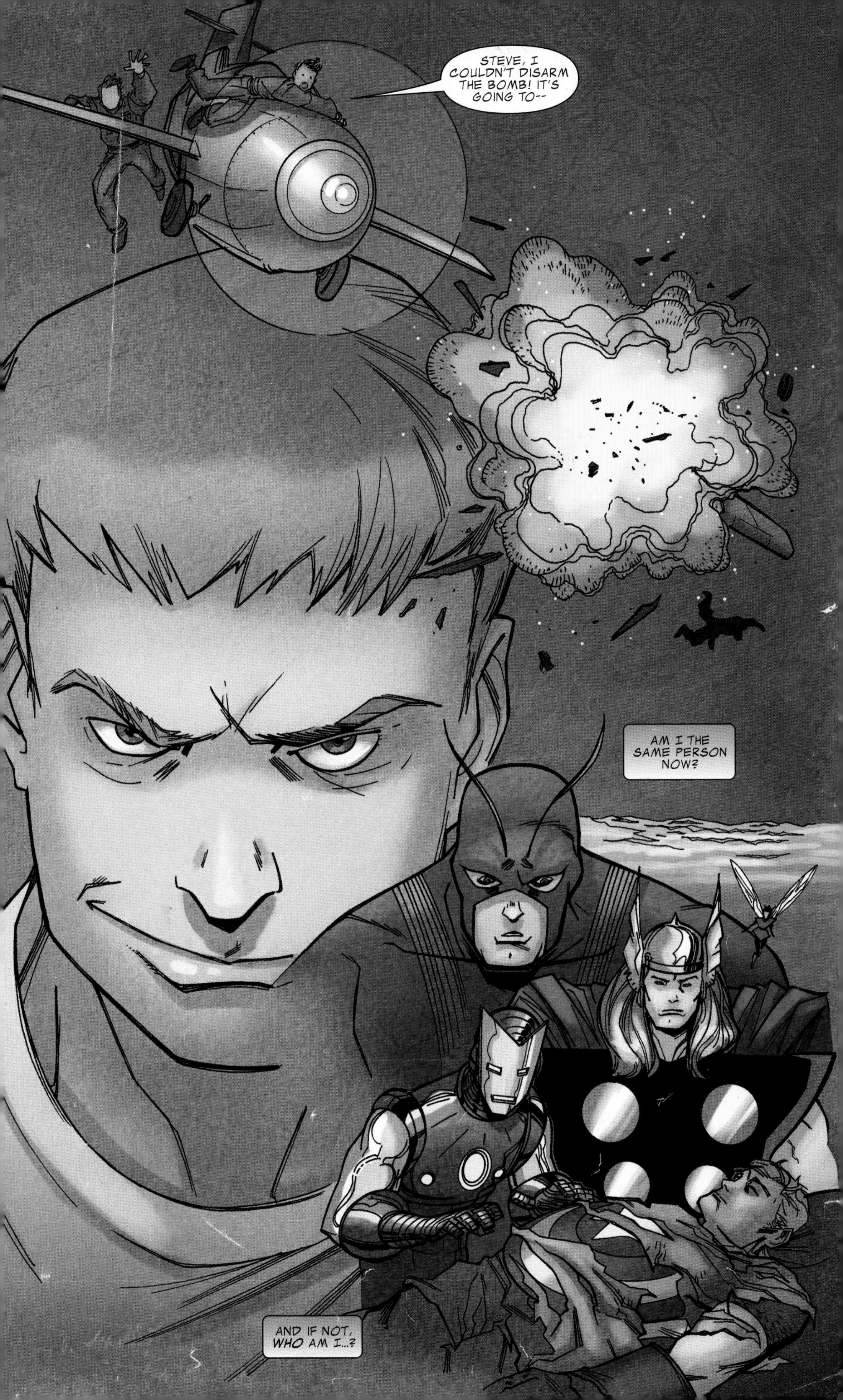
STEVE, I COULDN'T DISARM THE BOMB! IT'S GOING TO--
AM I THE SAME PERSON NOW?
AND IF NOT, WHO AM I...?

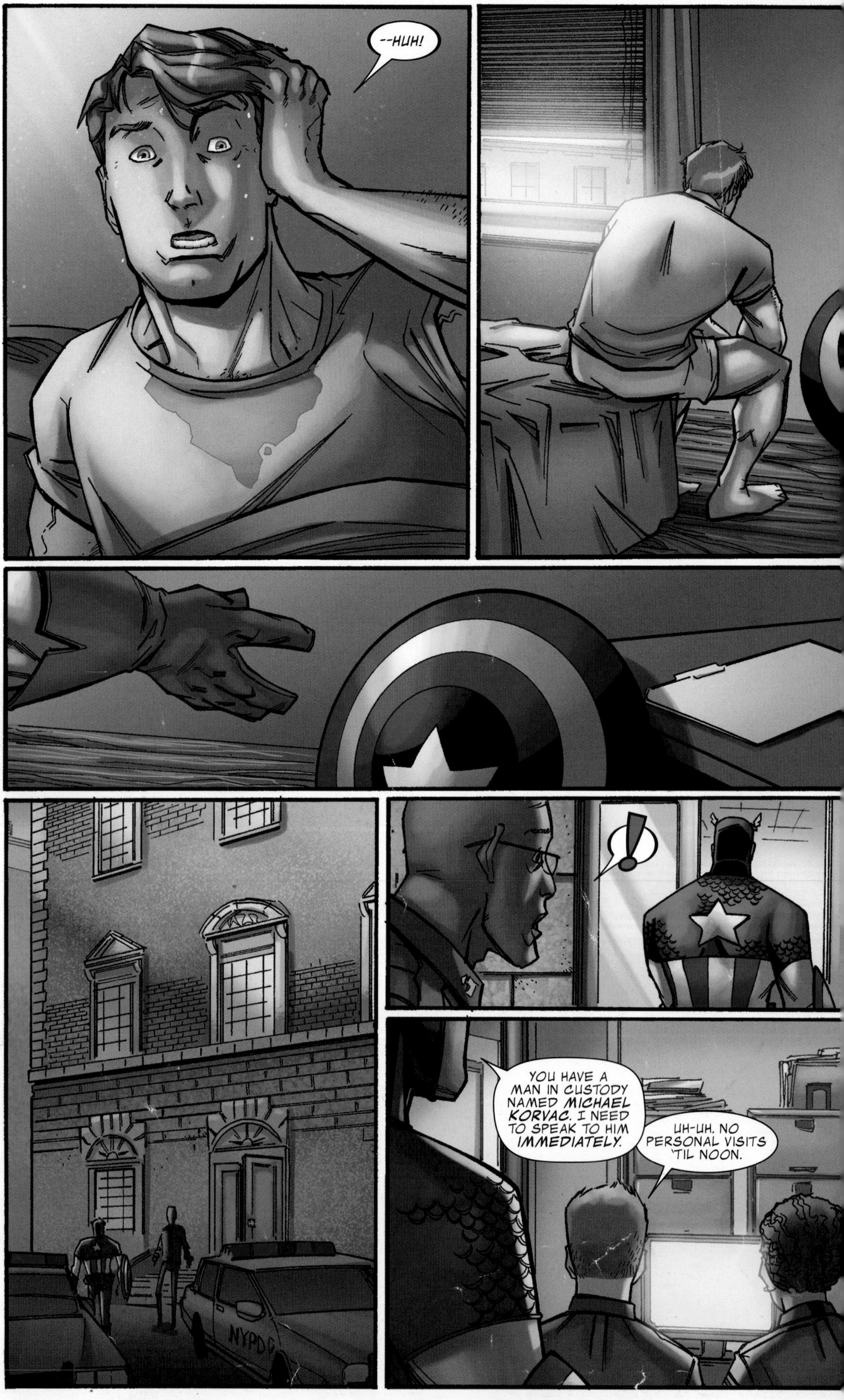
--HUH!
!
YOU HAVE A MAN IN CUSTODY NAMED MICHAEL KORVAC. I NEED TO SPEAK TO HIM IMMEDIATELY.
UH-UH. NO PERSONAL VISITS 'TIL NOON.
NYPD

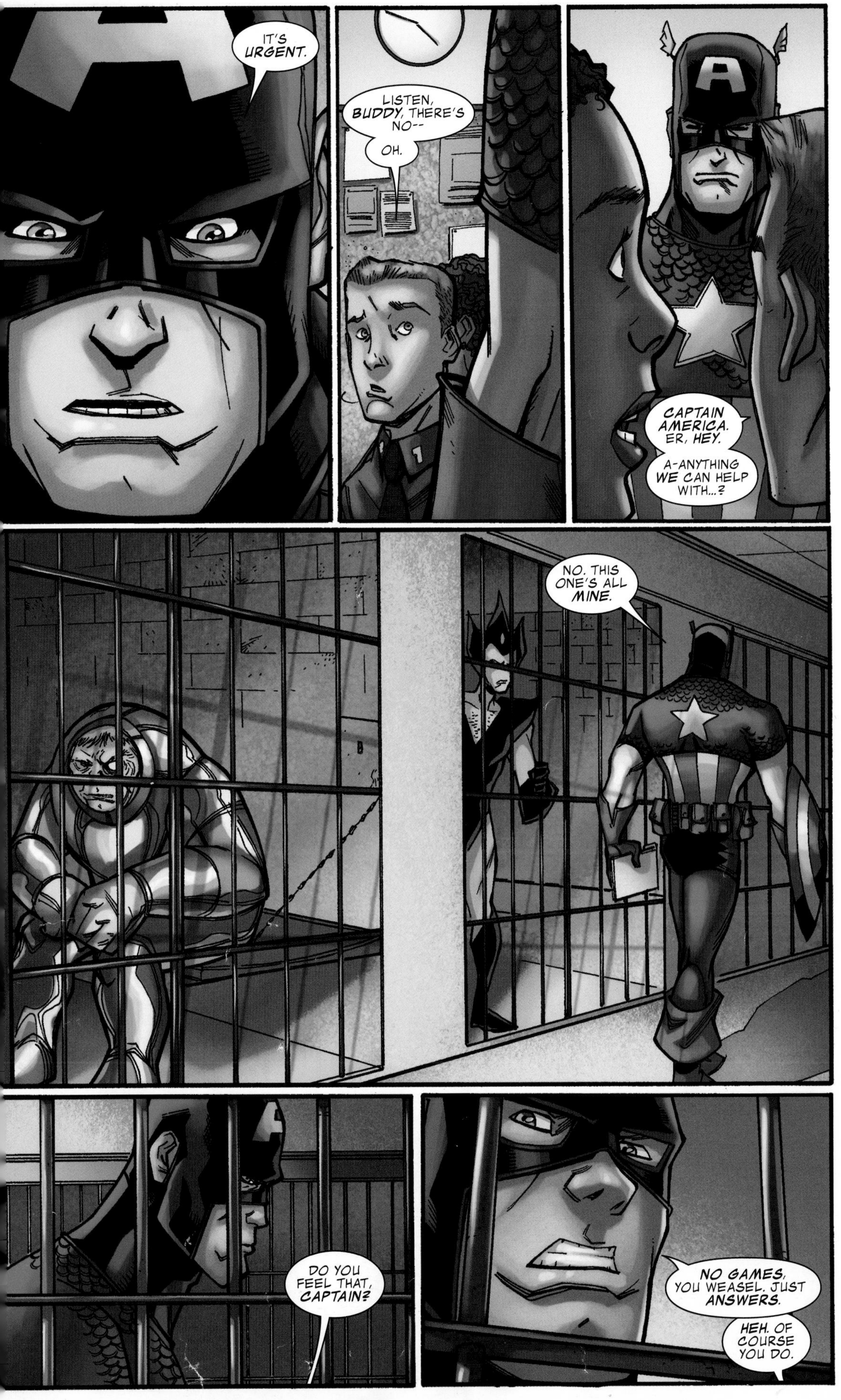
IT'S URGENT.
LISTEN, BUDDY, THERE'S NO--
OH.
CAPTAIN AMERICA. ER, HEY.
A-ANYTHING WE CAN HELP WITH...?
NO. THIS ONE'S ALL MINE.
DO YOU FEEL THAT, CAPTAIN?
NO GAMES, YOU WEASEL. JUST ANSWERS.
HEH. OF COURSE YOU DO.

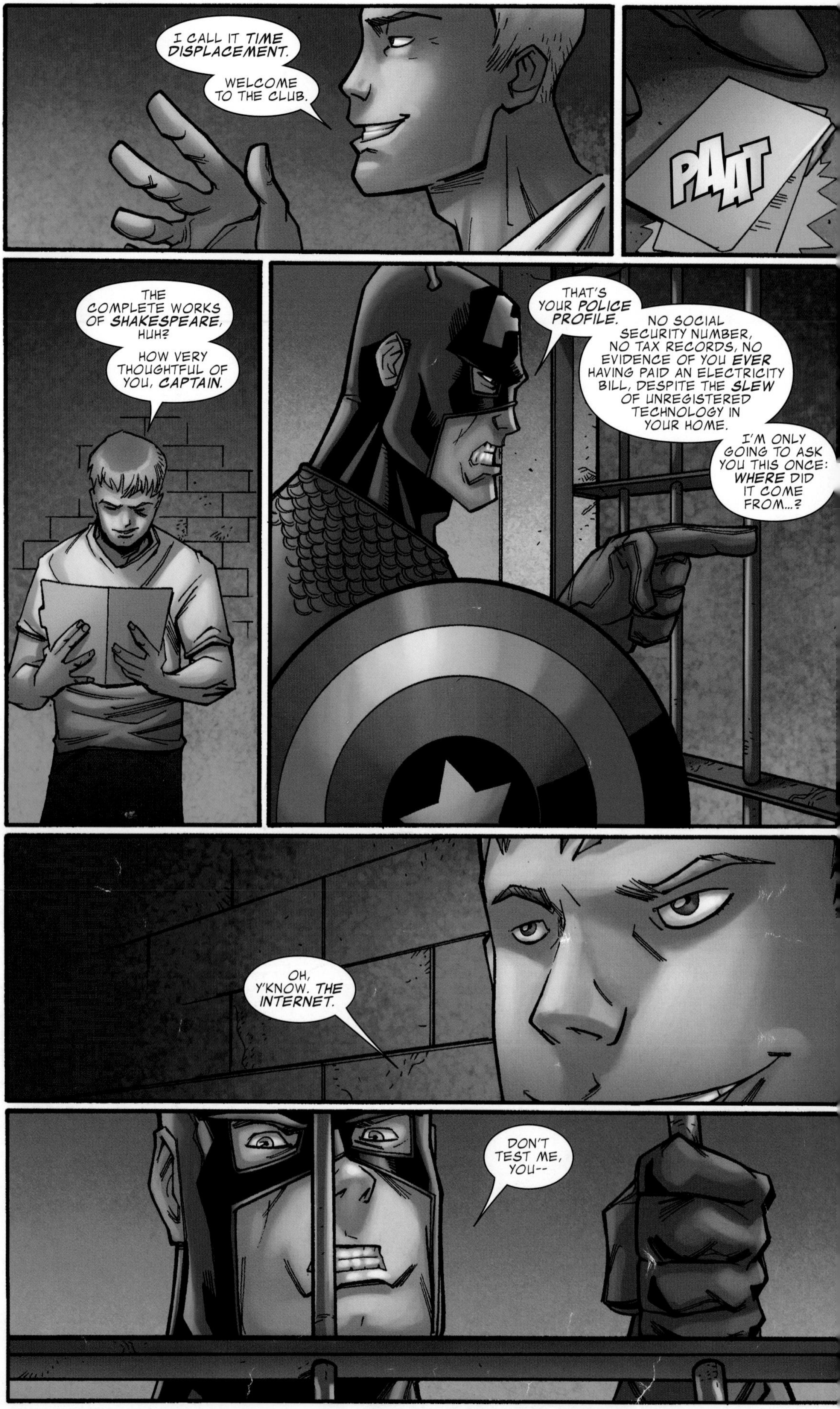
I CALL IT TIME DISPLACEMENT.
WELCOME TO THE CLUB.
PAAT
THE COMPLETE WORKS OF SHAKESPEARE, HUH?
HOW VERY THOUGHTFUL OF YOU, CAPTAIN.
THAT'S YOUR POLICE PROFILE.
NO SOCIAL SECURITY NUMBER, NO TAX RECORDS, NO EVIDENCE OF YOU EVER HAVING PAID AN ELECTRICITY BILL, DESPITE THE SLEW OF UNREGISTERED TECHNOLOGY IN YOUR HOME.
I'M ONLY GOING TO ASK YOU THIS ONCE: WHERE DID IT COME FROM...?
OH, Y'KNOW. THE INTERNET.
DON'T TEST ME, YOU--

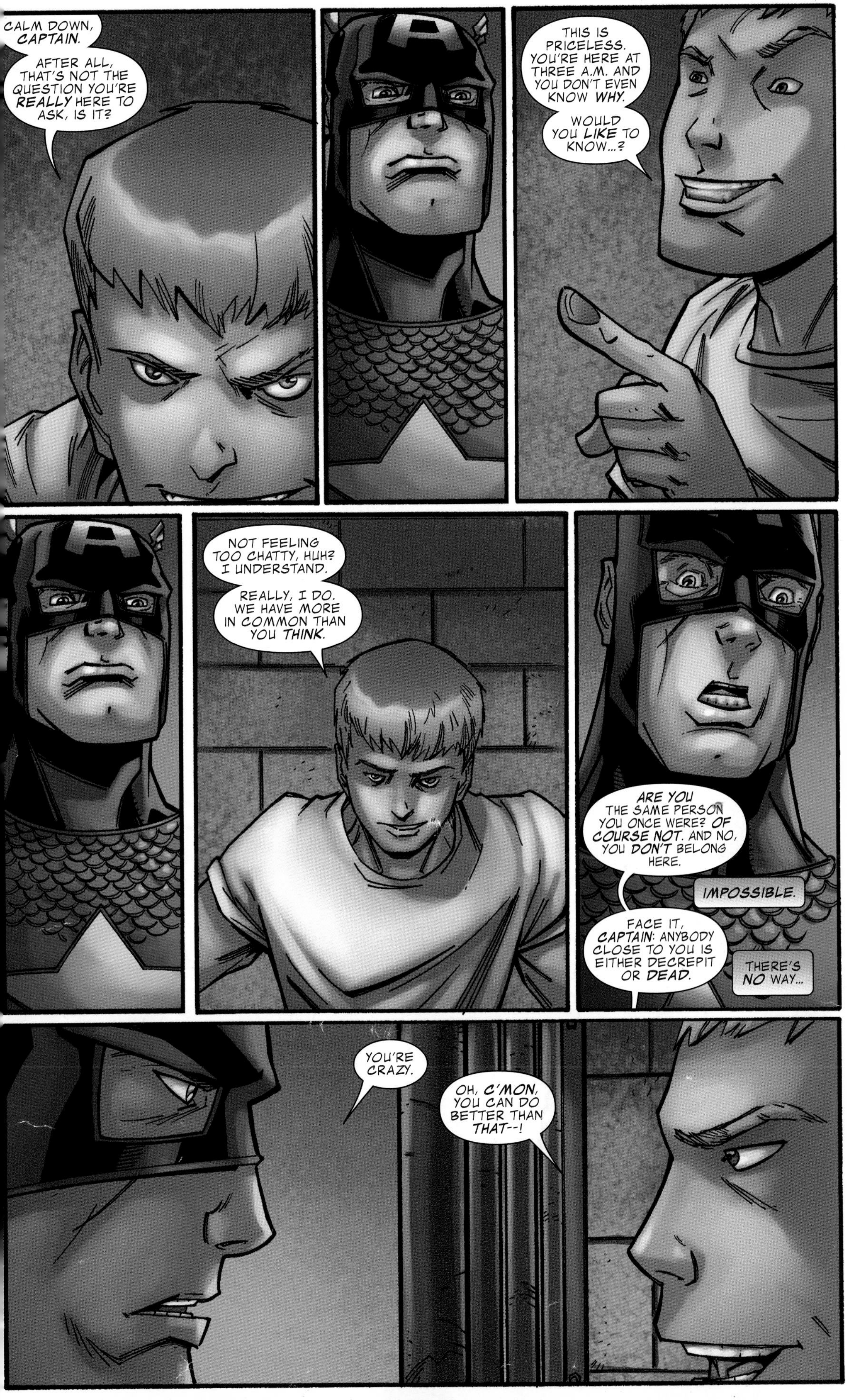
CALM DOWN, CAPTAIN.
AFTER ALL, THAT'S NOT THE QUESTION YOU'RE REALLY HERE TO ASK, IS IT?
THIS IS PRICELESS. YOU'RE HERE AT THREE A.M. AND YOU DON'T EVEN KNOW WHY.
WOULD YOU LIKE TO KNOW...?
NOT FEELING TOO CHATTY, HUH? I UNDERSTAND.
REALLY, I DO. WE HAVE MORE IN COMMON THAN YOU THINK.
ARE YOU THE SAME PERSON YOU ONCE WERE? OF COURSE NOT. AND NO, YOU DON'T BELONG HERE.
IMPOSSIBLE.
FACE IT, CAPTAIN: ANYBODY CLOSE TO YOU IS EITHER DECREPIT OR DEAD.
THERE'S NO WAY...
YOU'RE CRAZY.
OH, C'MON, YOU CAN DO BETTER THAN THAT--!

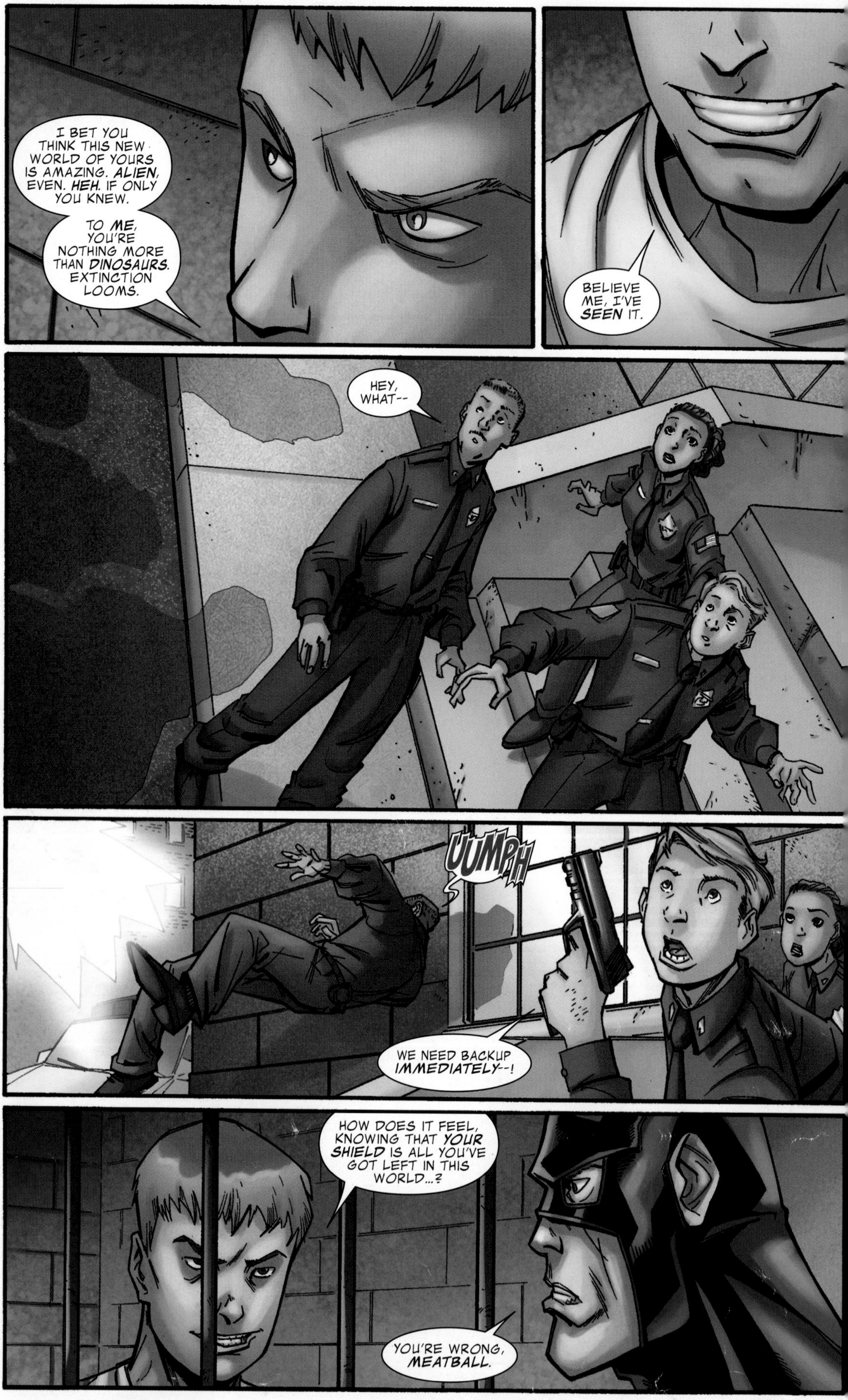
I BET YOU THINK THIS NEW WORLD OF YOURS IS AMAZING. ALIEN, EVEN. HEH. IF ONLY YOU KNEW.
TO ME, YOU'RE NOTHING MORE THAN DINOSAURS. EXTINCTION LOOMS.
BELIEVE ME, I'VE SEEN IT.
HEY, WHAT--
UUMPH
WE NEED BACKUP IMMEDIATELY--!
HOW DOES IT FEEL, KNOWING THAT YOUR SHIELD IS ALL YOU'VE GOT LEFT IN THIS WORLD...?
YOU'RE WRONG, MEATBALL.

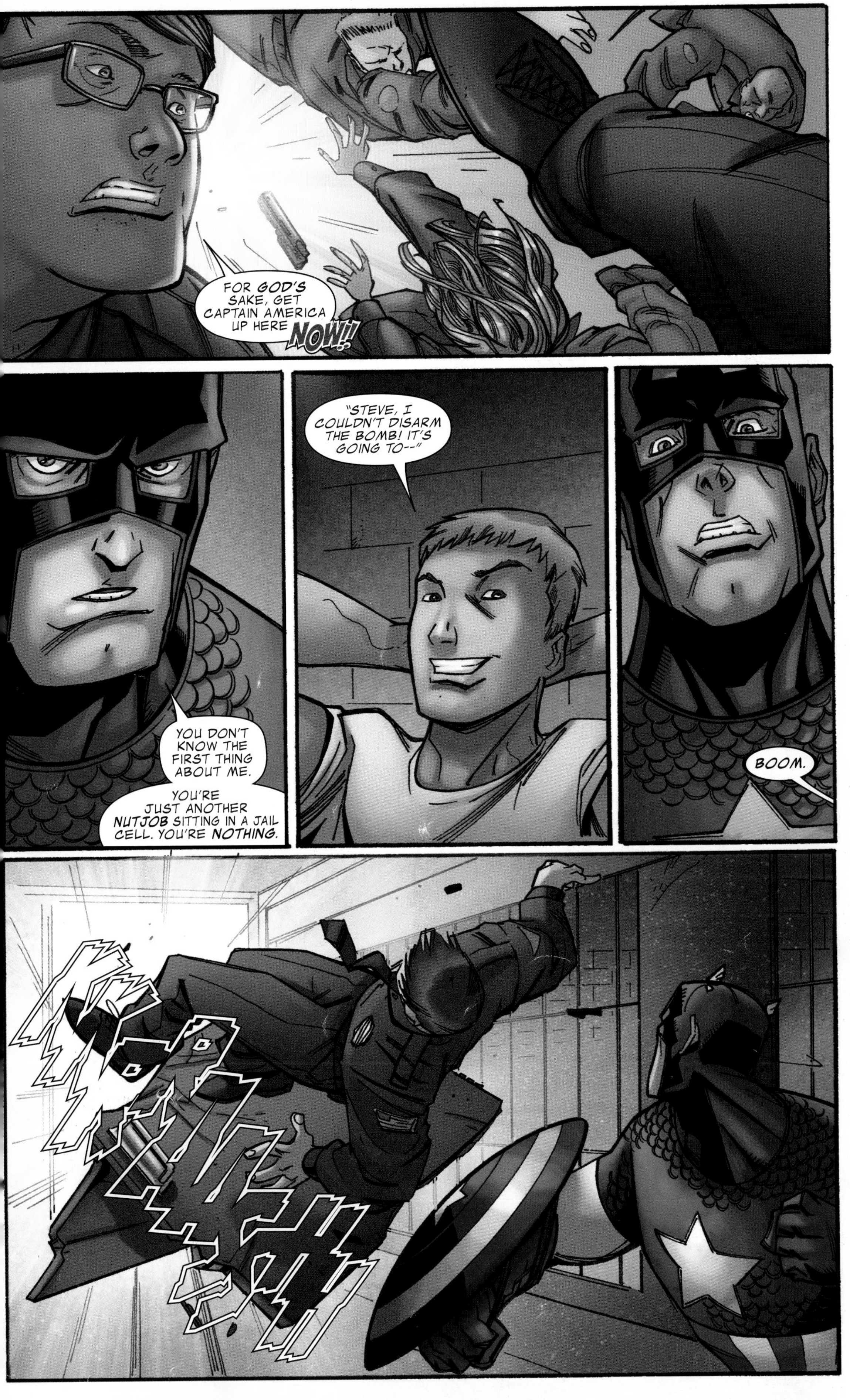

FOR GOD'S SAKE, GET CAPTAIN AMERICA UP HERE NOW!!
YOU DON'T KNOW THE FIRST THING ABOUT ME.
YOU'RE JUST ANOTHER NUTJOB SITTING IN A JAIL CELL. YOU'RE NOTHING.
"STEVE, I COULDN'T DISARM THE BOMB! IT'S GOING TO--"
BOOM.

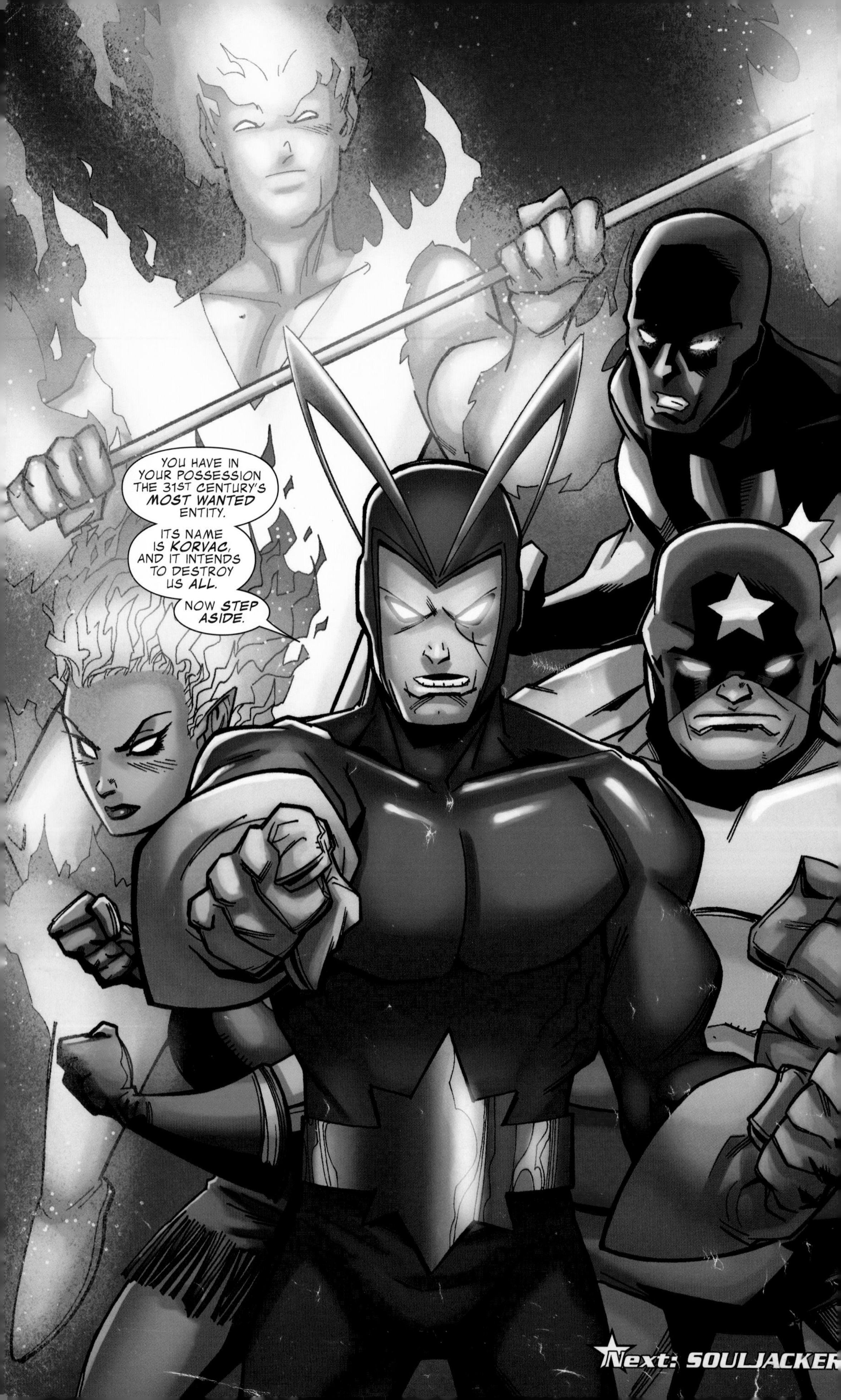
YOU HAVE IN YOUR POSSESSION THE 31ST CENTURY'S MOST WANTED ENTITY.
ITS NAME IS KORVAC, AND IT INTENDS TO DESTROY US ALL.
NOW STEP ASIDE.
Next: SOULJACKER